This book belongs to:

Contents

Cover illustration by Paula Martyr

Published by Ladybird Books Ltd
80 Strand London WC2R ORL
A Penguin Company

10 9

© LADYBIRD BOOKS LTD MCMXCVII, MMI

LADYBIRD and the device of a Ladybird are trademarks of Ladybird Books Ltd

Printed in China

The Wakey Wakey machine

written by Alan MacDonald
illustrated by Paula Martyr

Every morning, Jessie had trouble
waking up – even after her
four alarm clocks had gone off.

"It's no good," said her mum.
"This can't go on."

"There's only one thing for it," said
Dad. "She'll have to see Egon."

"Yes. Egon will know what to do,"
said Mum.

At last Jessie came downstairs.
Her mum handed her a mysterious-
looking envelope and told her
where to find Egon.

Jessie took the envelope to Egon's
house and pulled the doorbell.
The bell played some music, and the
door opened all by itself.
Inside was a small robot.
It had an egg-shaped head.

"Good morning. Welcome to Ideas Unlimited," it said.

Jessie looked around for someone else.

"I'm looking for Egon," she said. "This envelope is for him."

"I'm Egon," said the robot. "Please come this way."

Egon took Jessie into a big room that was full of amazing machines. "Where are all the people?" she asked.

"There aren't any," said Egon.

Machines of all kinds were
hurrying around busily.
Little lorries moved boxes, and
robots did the packing.
One robot was pouring
bright, fizzy drinks into cups.

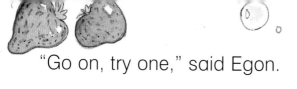

"Go on, try one," said Egon.

Jessie picked up a cup of red fizz.

"Mmm, it tastes like… like…
strawberries and cream."

"Exactly. That's just it," said Egon.
"We've also got banana and
chocolate cake flavours."

"But why?" said Jessie.

"Because fizzy orange is so
boring," said Egon.
"We have lots of other new ideas.
That's why we're called
Ideas Unlimited. Now let's have
a look at what's in your envelope."

Egon opened the envelope.
"Hmm. So you can't wake up
in the mornings."

"No," said Jessie.

"Then what you need is a
Wakey Wakey machine,"
said Egon.

"A Wakey Wakey machine?
What's that?" asked Jessie.

"I don't know. I haven't invented it
yet," said Egon. "But I'll soon
come up with something."

13

Next Monday morning, Jessie was fast asleep as usual.

Suddenly there was a whirr and a click. The weird machine by her bed had started working.

"Wakey, wakey, Jessie!" it boomed.

15

Loud music started to play. An arm came out and pulled Jessie's covers off her. Jessie groaned and turned over. But then her bed tipped up slowly and she fell onto the floor.

Jessie was suddenly awake.
The machine handed her a cup of
red fizz and put her slippers on.

"Mmm… strawberries and cream!"
said Jessie. "This is great."

17

She ran to her mum and dad's
bedroom.

"Come and see the Wakey Wakey
machine! It worked!"

But when Jessie opened the door…
Mum and Dad were still fast asleep
and snoring loudly.

Bambang and his ducks

written and illustrated by
Elizabeth St.John

Bambang was pleased.
He and Sri had spent all day
making their new kite.
Now it was ready for flying.

"Let's try it out," said Bambang.

"No, not yet, or we'll be in trouble,"
said Sri. "First you must go
to collect the ducks and I must
make their feed."

"Oh, do I have to?" said Bambang.

"Yes, you do," insisted Sri.
"Go on. Hurry!"

Bambang ran as fast as
he could to the paddy fields
to find the ducks.

When Bambang whistled for
the ducks, they waddled up,
quacking loudly.

"Is everyone here?" asked Bambang, counting them quickly. "Good. Let's go."

Bambang and the ducks set off for the house.

Sri was waiting with the feed for the ducks. She counted them as they waddled up to her.

"Bambang, one duck is missing!
There are only nineteen!" she cried.

"No, count again, Sri.
They must all be here.
Look, there are twenty."

Bambang insisted on counting
them for himself. But Sri was
right. One duck was missing.

"You must go back to find it.
Hurry, hurry, it's getting late,"
Sri insisted. "Soon it will be
dark and we won't have time
to fly our kite."

Bambang was worried. He ran back
to the paddy fields as fast as he
could and called loudly.

He looked by the river.
Maybe the water rats were
bullying the missing duck?

But no, the water rats were
playing happily.

Bambang whistled a second
time and looked on the ground.
Maybe the snake was trying
to eat the missing duck?

But no, the snake was sleeping
quietly.

Bambang whistled a third time
and looked in the trees.
Maybe the monkeys were teasing
the missing duck?

But no, the monkeys were eating
noisily.

Just then Bambang heard
a quiet little quack. It was
the missing duck! It had been
hiding in the paddy fields
all along.

"How did I miss you? You'll be
all right, now I've found you,"
said Bambang quietly.
"Let's take you home."

Now Sri and Bambang could take their kite out and fly it with their friends. And their kite went higher and stayed up for longer than all the others. It was the best kite ever.

Windy nights

from a poem by Robert Louis Stevenson
illustrated by Trevor Parkin

Whenever the moon and stars are set,

Whenever the wind is high,

All night long in the dark and wet,

A man goes riding by.

Late in the night when the lights are out,

Why does he gallop and gallop about?